THANK YOU FOR BEING WITH US

THOMAS HEERMA VAN VOSS

TRANSLATION BY / *VERTALING DOOR*
MOSHE GILULA

Thank You For Being With Us
by Thomas Heerma van Voss

Translated from the Dutch
by Moshe Gilula

First published in English
by Strangers Press, Norwich, 2020,
(part of UEA Publishing Project)

Distributed
by NBN International

Printed
by Swallowtail Print, Norwich

All rights reserved
© *Thomas Heerma van Voss, 2020,*
published by Thomas Rap Publishers
Translation
© *Moshe Gilula, 2020,*
mentored by Sam Garrett

Editorial team
Nathan Hamilton, David Colmer,
Michele Hutchison, Bas Pauw and Victor Schiferli

Editorial assistance
by Senica Maltese

Cover design and typesetting
by Office of Craig

Main body text is set using Arnhem,
Headings are set in Nord

The rights of Thomas Heerma van Voss to be identified as the author and Moshe Gilula to be identified as the translator of this work have been asserted in accordance with the Copyright, Designs and Patents Act, 1988. This booklet is sold subject to the condition that it shall not, by way of trade or otherwise, be lent, resold, hired out, stored in a retrieval system, or otherwise circulated without the publisher's prior consent in any form of binding or cover other than that in which it is published and without a similar condition including this condition being imposed on the subsequent purchaser.

ISBN-13: 978-1911343288

Thank You For Being With Us

CONTENTS

THE MASSAGE PARLOR 5

THANK YOU FOR BEING WITH US 13

strangers press

THE MASSAGE PARLOR

For four months now I've been living across from an erotic massage parlour. It's a narrow building, four storeys high. The curtains are drawn day and night. All you can see from the outside is the space behind the glass front door, where there's always a young, seductive woman in a short, tight-fitting dress. I know that at least seven ladies work there, all dark-haired, most of them Asian. But I never see more than one behind the door, they keep taking turns. Possibly because one woman looks more enticing than a group of them. This gives every man who walks by the feeling that someone is waiting especially for him. That the massage parlour is there just for him.

There's a sign above the entrance: LOVE MASSAGE. The customers go in alone, then come out alone after no more than an hour. They usually look around sheepishly, tired too, sometimes even exhausted. One time a client collapsed at the door, panting, his skin glistening. Passersby eyed him in bewilderment, but no one bothered to speak to him. Then one of the massage parlour women came outside. 'Can you please go away?' Her voice resonated through the alley. 'You have to get up. You have to go.' Slowly the man got up. The woman shooed him away as if he were a stray dog. If you ask me, she couldn't have cared less if he got a heart attack and dropped dead, as long as it wasn't in front of the massage parlour.

To get in you have to ring the bell. No matter how affably the woman behind the door smiles at you, no matter how long and how benevolently you look back at her: nothing will happen unless you press the bell. When I was new to the neighbourhood, I wondered whether this was costing the massage parlour clients. Now I think I get the strategy. The women put the responsibility in the customer's hands. They give him an active role in the game right away — because that's what it is, after all; a game of seduction. Letting the client make the first move makes him feel he's the one taking the initiative, that he's the seducer, not the one being seduced.

The door doesn't open right after the bell has been rung. First there's the price-list. The woman produces it from behind her back, on Mondays and Tuesdays even from under her dress: a laminated sheet of paper with big, pink letters. Without saying anything the woman presses the list against the door, for no more than a few seconds. Then she folds it back up and looks enticingly at the potential client. It took me days to work out the whole list.

massages + body 30 min € 50
Massages + body 50 min €90
Massages+ sex + Body 30 min € 75
Massages +Sex + Body 50 min € 135

The fixed-price menu gets pressed against the door dozens of times a day. And no matter how often I see it, it still baffles me. Are all the missing spaces intentional? Is the first *m* lowercase in order to discourage choosing that option? Is *Sex* deliberately capitalised only in the most expensive category? Does the parlour's owner realise that €135 for fifty minutes is a worse deal than €75 for thirty minutes?

I'm probably the only one who even pays any attention to all this. The men who come that close to the door have other things on their mind. They are startled by the sheet of paper behind the glass, fantasise about what can happen in there, consider how much money they'd be willing to spend, tops. That's why, even after the list disappears, they stay put for a few more seconds: they observe the woman behind the door, try to deduce something from her behaviour. But the woman does nothing but smile. If the customer turns around, it's like nothing happened, he can just walk on and pretend he was only looking. But if he stays there long enough, then steps forward, it's game on. He can still go through the motions, as if he's hesitating, try to decide which of the four options he'll choose, check just to be sure he has the cash, maybe even think up an alibi in case of inconvenient inquiries later in the evening. But as soon as he rings the bell it's clear he's going to pay and be back on the street within an hour, satiated.

No one can see me. My room is on the first floor. I'm lying on my bed, looking outside. My sheets smell of sweat. But what do I care, I'm the only one who can smell it.

There's a notepad on my lap, at the top it says: LOVE MASSAGE. I note down a lot more about the parlour than just the price-list. It started as a simple pastime during my first few weeks living here. My TV wasn't working yet, my internet was on the blink, I wasn't in the mood for company and studying all day wasn't an option. With two pillows tucked behind my back, I gazed at the massage parlour. I'd never seen such a hectic and lively business from up close. There were no shops or workplaces on the street where I grew up, just identical houses, block after block.

I started by counting how many customers come to the massage parlour every evening. At least fifty, more than a hundred on weekends. I wanted exact numbers and would make a mark in my notebook for each customer that rang the bell. Then I would try to imagine each one's age and occupation. I was already looking, why not make it more interesting for myself? I ended up inventing complete stories about them. The stories told themselves; without my noticing it, all sorts of details ended up on paper: where the customer lived, whether he had a partner, perhaps even children. Whether he paid for company more often. I devoted more pages to the most striking clients. These were precious moments in which I let myself get carried away, everything that popped into my head went to my notepad.

About a long-haired young man on a rental bike, I wrote: *Born mid-eighties in a small Norwegian village. His parents worked for a large oil company, so had to move constantly. In every new town the boy had to live in he tried to impress his classmates with grandiose stories. He invented all kinds of adventures, which he would embellish each time they moved. Today he's a screenwriter, target audience unknown. He was turned down by the film academy in Munich twice. He's going to try again next year. Now he's doing research in the Netherlands though he's not really sure for what.*

About a middle-aged man in a black suit and slick sunglasses: *Comes from Texas, happily married since college. Has had a humdrum job at a prison for years, but he's OK about it. This is his first — and probably last — time in Europe. He's going to Paris tomorrow, Berlin the day after, then he's flying back to America. Sundays he likes to drink beer and watch football. Likes driving around in his Ford and watching action movies starring Nicolas Cage; two kids, a dog, an attractive house with a garden.*

The writing gave me an exceptional sense of fulfilment every time. All those people, all those lives: on paper I ruled over them. Sometimes I would sit at my desk and write stories based on my notes. I would add details, make up scenes, write dialogues, and although I wouldn't show anything I wrote to anyone, it was liberating, the power I got from making things up. I didn't have to worry about whether I was doing a good job and about what other people would think. I would look out the window, see the chaotic, urban life and I'd decide which life story went with which face, who was hiding the deepest secrets, what fate had in store for them. And no one had a thing to say about it.

The massage parlour doesn't have regular customers. The visitors are almost exclusively foreigners. Travelling businessmen who need something to do in the evening, tourist friends challenging each other. 'Get a massage, I'll pay.' The shrill voices sound up and down the alley. 'You're always so yellow, this time you're gonna do it.' I heard such phrases countless times; always spoken as if they were so original. What follows is always the same, too: dilly-dallying, laughter, more dilly-dallying, and eventually one of the guys goes in. While he's being treated his friends wait outside. They smoke a joint, pee on the wall, play with their phones. On rare occasions they say something, in English or in a language I don't understand. The conversations are never lengthy. Once in a while, after a few minutes, one of them suggests going for ice cream, probably on the Nieuwmarkt. Then I see the group amble out the alley and after a while show up again in front of the parlour, wiping their sticky hands on their pants. Sometimes they just sit, backs against a door or a wall, waiting in silence till the purchased pleasures a few steps away are over.

When the parlour door opens they all get up at once. High fives are exchanged, shoulders are slapped, questions asked. 'And, was it good?' 'Was it worth the money?' The client usually smiles roguishly, even though his body language doesn't reveal any signs of enthusiasm. He gives them the thumbs-up or starts in on a detailed description of what happened inside, but I can never make that out because as soon as the friends are reunited, they walk out of the alley and therefore out of my life forever, as nameless as they entered it an hour ago.

There's one man I see at the massage parlour on a regular basis: the owner. At least, I assume he's the owner because every day one of the women hands him a visibly full envelope. Now he's here for the second time this afternoon. A bald man in his forties on a scooter you can hear approaching from afar. As usual he's carrying two garbage bags. It's unclear what they contain: clothes, towels, maybe water bottles for his workers? Of course he may also be bringing romantic candles or oil for massaging the customers with. All I see is the owner ringing the bell and putting the garbage bags next to the door without getting off his scooter. Then he's handed the envelope, which he promptly puts into his inner pocket. He doesn't say a word. He doesn't look at anyone. Every time he comes to the parlour he does exactly the same things; I know his gestures, his impatient manner, his blank expression.

In my notebook I jot down: *2:54 p.m. Owner brings garbage bags.* I reread the words twice and wonder whether I could write a story about him — interesting, actually, a massage parlour owner, how does someone end up in this business, why does he keep on doing it, day in, day out? On the other hand: it's such a stereotype, a bald, stolid man on a scooter. If I write about him shouldn't I give him a completely different character, younger, more remarkable?

Without deciding I put down my notebook. I need to get a move on. My class starts at three. A study group. I'll probably be a few minutes late, when the teacher is already in class, but before her lesson has begun. She'll give me a reprimanding look but say nothing. I'll sit in the back. None of the other students will say anything to me, I won't start any conversations. To the one question I'll be asked, about some theory or article I've never heard of, I'll improvise an answer. I'll nod understandingly when the teacher says I should prepare more thoroughly. I'll take notes, write down every word that's spoken so I won't have to listen.

But maybe I'll call in sick and stay here the rest of the day, safe behind my window.

Saturdays are always the busiest at Love Massage. I write ten sheets-full, easy, then read it in bed at night, with a feeling of satisfaction.

I used to admire adults, who seemed to know exactly how to lead their lives and what was demanded of them in all circumstances. I thought: I have to be patient, my young years are only a warming up, one day I'll be one of the adults and know how to behave too. But now I understand that the warming up isn't that different from the real match. I don't feel myself getting older, it's just that I see more and more young people around me. I don't see my peers gradually working toward a perfect job or a care-free marriage. They end up in a random office or company, where, without giving it a second thought, they sell their most energetic hours for an average rate; they go to bed with a stranger who gets them a beer at a house party, they develop a relationship with the person who listens most patiently to their stories, and of all their friends, the one who is still single in his or her early thirties has the greatest chance of becoming their children's parent.

But when I read my notes in the middle of the night, I can forget all that, for a moment the future is insignificant.

Last weekend I was lying down, restfully looking out the window, when suddenly my mother knocked on my door. It was the first time in weeks anyone had dropped by. She had a bag full of groceries. Strawberries, juice, milk, she put it all into the refrigerator. Then she wiped the counter with a rag and opened the window. 'It's been sunny all week, why don't you go out and get some fresh air?'

I shook my head and we talked about general stuff. That they don't make any good movies nowadays, that more and more men have a beard, that this summer she and my father are going on vacation to Italy. Then I lied about having to do an assignment for school. She nodded understandingly, stood up, but hesitated at the door and suddenly looked at me earnestly. 'You know you're always welcome home?' she asked. 'It's great that you managed to find a room here, right in the city centre, but we hardly hear from you any more. If you want a break from all the bustle you could always come stay with us for a couple of days, you know.' She stopped speaking for a few seconds. I heard the door of the massage parlour fall shut. It depressed me not to be able to see who had left or had gone in. 'You don't have to tell us everything, you know,' my mother said. 'But a smidgeon of information once in a while would be nice.'

    I obviously could have told her how I spend most of my time, that I write and wait, wait and write, but how could I explain it convincingly? Besides my mother wasn't really worried, I could see it in her eyes. Even if I said nothing she'd bike home without a care, away from her child who is now living alone. She'd talk about me proudly in her yoga class, her friends would hear unsolicited accounts of how well I was doing. She believes in me. Like everyone around me, in fact. Teachers, family, acquaintances — no one had ever thought I wouldn't amount to anything.

It's two minutes after midnight. The owner has just brought two fresh garbage bags and picked up his envelope. A slim, dark-skinned man is standing in front of the massage parlour. He's wearing flip-flops and carrying a threadbare The North Face backpack. Where is he from? He looks like someone who's been through a lot. Sunken cheeks, a scar on his chin.

    12:02 a.m. New potential customer. About 35. Born in Nigeria, exact date of birth unknown. For a long time he dreamed of becoming a star athlete, now works as an online businessman, not exactly clear in what. Moves each year, now living in Amsterdam. Expected more from the Red Light District: better-looking women, more people. But still doesn't want to deprive himself, if for no other reason than that he was so triumphant about announcing to his friends that he would go there.

    I see the man take the last few steps toward the door. Slowly, almost reluctantly. He looks around. There's no one else in the alley. Almost all the curtains are drawn. Most of the light is coming from the LOVE MASSAGE sign. Behind the glass, a young woman is smiling at him. I've seen her on the job before; I know how she wins over her customers. By first blinking her eyes innocently, then gradually starting to grin. The dark-skinned man plays along fully, probably without realising it. He makes eye contact, slows down, scans the area again. Almost fifteen minutes go by before he finally rings the bell with a seducer's swank.

12:14 a.m. The price-list appears. I think the man will go for the full treatment, he'll do anything to make the high expectations he had of the District come true. So: Sex with a capital S.

There's no other place I'd rather be than here, alone on my bed. I look at my notes with satisfaction, the biography I just jotted down, all those other biographies. When I go outside I'll discover where I didn't get it right, I'll find out how many of my notes don't make any sense, how useless my made-up stories are, but as long as I stay in bed, I'm the one who decides what the truth is.

12:48 a.m. I don't think he really enjoyed it. He walks off, head bowed and shoulders drooping. But his evening isn't over yet, he won't allow it. He goes to a coffee shop, looking for relaxation. He takes a picture of his joint and sends it to a couple of friends, hoping to make them jealous. In the future he will have children but will never marry or have a relationship that lasts more than a couple of years.

I close my eyes, listen to the tourists walking by and hear the massage parlour door open again. Sometimes I fantasise that it's my door. That all the customers come to see me, that every day dozens of people think I'm worth visiting and that someone else is watching me closely. Then I look at my notes and think: yes, these people are part of me.

I hear footsteps, heavy and emphatic, followed by a few halting words in English. The door falls shut. Right now the woman behind the glass is probably holding up her hand for the money. Yes, I know for sure, I don't need to open my eyes and check. The customer, excited but also nervous, wallet in hand; facing him, the woman. Made-up face, pampered skin, breasts accentuated by her dress. Like all the other girls, she knows exactly what to do now. How long to keep smiling, how to earn the money as quickly as possible, how to tempt and seduce.

Can they see me from where they're standing? And if they did, would they smile at me too?

THANK YOU FOR BEING WITH US

Egbert's son had written a thesis on domestic violence. The thesis became a book, the book became a bestseller and Egbert's son became an authority on dysfunctional families. Every time a teen mom loses it and poisons her child, a stressed-out househusband maims his wife or an unresponsive teenager stabs his parents, Koen is invited to appear on TV and explain, in carefully formulated sentences that everyone can understand, how such a thing could happen.

Egbert never intended to become a father. Children slobber and whine and demand constant attention, Marieke thought so too. So they took precautions. Condoms. The pill. Their doctor said: Chances of pregnancy in such cases are less than 0.1%. Egbert still remembers the cold spring day, when Marieke and he heard those words. He'd insisted they go see the doctor. Just to be on the safe side. He remembers leaving the surgery in Amsterdam West, straightening his collar and thinking: Why didn't he just round it off to 0%? It's such a negligible difference. Now he knows. Koen is living proof that less than 0.1% isn't the same as 0%.

The last time Egbert was in the Netherlands was years ago. Sitting next to him, on the train from Brussels, is a young woman with a ponytail. She occasionally looks at him inquisitively and leafs through a magazine. On one of the last pages Egbert sees his son's face flash by. It startles him. Maybe because the photo is so unexpected. Maybe he had secretly hoped his son would look older now, more like himself. But Koen looks as boyish as ever. Not a trace of the beginnings of baldness, nothing that even remotely resembles wrinkles or a slight double chin. *Tonight, 8:30, live: an interview with the Argentinian author A. Rosada about his drug addiction, and 28-year-old bestselling author Koen Talan in a head-to-head talk with his father about their tumultuous...*
The woman turns the page. Tumultuous what? Past? Relationship?

The central station is cold and busy. Egbert had taken a late train in order to avoid the rush hour, but even now, just before seven, it's full of people. He doesn't look at anyone and drags his heavy suitcase behind him like a recalcitrant dog. Why in heaven's name did he pack so many clothes?

Every couple of steps he halts to make sure he's going the right way. When he travels out of Brussels Alma always comes with him. She knows exactly where to go and alerts him if he goes the wrong way. But this time Egbert heard himself saying to her: 'Stay home. Why should you spend hours in the train during Christmas? Anyway, I'll be back tomorrow.'

Lately she's been complaining that he just lets things happen. That life is passing him by. If she could see him now, surrounded by all these people, charting out his own route, she'd realise how ridiculous her claims are.

Two doors slide open. Egbert walks out of the station, through a group of tourists, and crosses a bridge. The snow crunches under his feet. On the corner of the Singel a dark BMW is waiting, as agreed. The chauffeur is a young Moroccan with shiny, spiky hair. 'Mr. Talan, glad you could make it.' The chauffeur doesn't introduce himself. 'We have just enough time to drive by the hotel. You have to be in the studio in forty-five minutes.'

They drive into the city, past squares and grand houses. In many of the living rooms there are Christmas trees, decorated and lit, sometimes surrounded by children. Egbert looks around restlessly. The years he lived here seem unreal to him now, as if he had dreamed them and all that remains of those dreams are vague shreds.

He turns away from the car window, stares at his hands, his arms, his belly, and wonders what the public will see when he comes on.

'We're here,' the chauffeur says.

They're in front of a three-star hotel, close to Leidseplein. The chauffeur gets out, opens the passenger door and rolls Egbert's suitcase to the entrance.

Egbert has no choice but to follow. In the lobby there are two plastic palm trees and, hanging on the wall, a painted portrait of the king. The woman behind the counter smiles when she sees Egbert. 'Ah, Mr. Talan, you finally arrived. How nice.' She doesn't have to check his name or whether he has a reservation. Tonight everything has been taken care of.

'Your son said there was a good chance you wouldn't show up,' the woman says. 'Or if you did that you'd be very late. So he's already checked you in, you can go straight to your room.'

Egbert's hotel room is much larger than his bedroom at home. There's a box of chocolates on the bed. *Welcome to our show,* it says, signed by a network CEO. Egbert washes his hands and opens the window. He sees the BMW that brought him on the other side of the street. The headlights are shining brightly and, by the sound of it, the motor is still running. At first Egbert thinks: Why doesn't the car just drive off, what's he hanging around for? Then it occurs to him that the chauffeur has been instructed to wait for him, he won't do anything till tonight's guest comes outside.

Egbert takes a long, hot shower. He uses all the soaps and shampoos on the sink. He feels a short, burning sensation in his stomach, the same as he sometimes gets at work just before a performance review. He hasn't eaten enough — only a pre-packaged chicken sandwich at Roosendaal station. Why is he even participating in this show? He's never been on television before. During the preliminary interview on the phone — a young woman's voice asked questions, such as: 'How would you describe your relationship with your son?' and: 'Would you have preferred your son to have chosen a completely different occupation?' — he kept asking himself what they saw in him. Whether he had anything TV-worthy to say. No one had ever taken the trouble to interview him, not in Amsterdam, not in Voorschoten. Not even for his department's internal bulletin. But still, hundreds of thousands of people are about to watch, several cameras are already waiting for him.

It was more than three weeks ago that Koen had sent him an email in the middle of the night. The last time they had had any contact was seven months before, Koen had just turned twenty-eight. Egbert always called his son on his birthday. The conversations were mostly businesslike and would peter out within a few minutes and repeat themselves in the same chilly tone a year later.

Dear father, Koen wrote, *I have an important request.* His son's formal tone didn't surprise Egbert. At most he thought it was strange that Koen had written him at all. He read the message twice but registered only disconnected words. Interview. Christmas special. Commercial channel. Two authors, the Argentinian and Koen, but only if he would come with his father.

Dear son, how are you? Egbert emailed back. He was disappointed not to be able to come up with a better text. *Let's take our time and talk about it, preferably on the phone. I doubt whether my presence is necessary. After all, you do everything (not to mention this book) all by yourself, right?*

His email didn't result in a phone call, Koen sent an even more peremptory message. *Bestseller. Promotion opportunity. Be helpful for once. I'll do the hotel, change of scenery.* And the same day, in a burst of decisiveness or cowardice, of fatherly responsibility or fear of even less contact, Egbert gave in.

In the evening he said to Alma as offhandedly as he could: 'I'll be on Dutch TV next week.'

The phone rings. Egbert quickly gets out of the shower. Brief joy: Ah, Koen wants to drive down to the studio together, or Alma is calling to wish me luck. But he quickly realises it's not his cell phone but the hotel's. The chauffeur is asking what's taking so long. 'You know they're expecting us at the studio now? You were only supposed to bring up your luggage.'

Egbert dries himself off hastily in the middle of the room. He digs through his suitcase, chooses his fanciest shirt and goes downstairs. The chauffeur is waiting for him in the lobby, grinning. Egbert gives a friendly nod in return. He knows it's only part of the job. Smile, show no impatience or irritation. Next month the driver will do the same with another guest, after a few shows he'll have no idea any more who Egbert is, but now Talan Sr. is the centre of attention, he will provide the spectacle people are longing for.

They turn onto the Nassaukade. On the radio a man is talking excitedly about something controversial some American politician had said. After that they play a number by an American band. The bass echoes in Egbert's stomach and distracts him briefly. For a few seconds he stops thinking about Amsterdam, about Koen or the broadcast, for a moment he feels just fine and he's simply an anonymous person listening to the radio in a random car.

'Are you nervous?' the chauffeur asks.

Egbert thinks. 'Now? Or in general?'

'About tonight, of course.'

Egbert shakes his finger, way too nonchalant, like someone who's on TV every week.

He texts Alma. *Doing OK honey? I am. Good hotel, friendly people. On way to studio, show starting soon. Gonna watch? xxx.*

'It makes sense,' the chauffeur says after a silence. 'That you're nervous, I mean. It's national TV, right? I think I'll watch when I get home right after this. I'm curious about your story.'

'Me too,' says Egbert. Streets and canals flash by, empty taxis, spacious homes. He sees his vague reflection in the side window. 'Me too.'

The TV studio is located in an old factory. At the entrance a blonde in her early thirties is waiting for Egbert. She introduces herself as the production assistant and leads him to the dressing room, where they quickly and perfunctorily powder him up. 'Your face is totally different than your son's,' he hears, as the brush fleets over his cheeks. And a bit later: 'Of course we don't have much time but we really have to get rid of those flakes on your nose. That's what you get with this weather, know what I mean?'

In the hallway men and women are walking up and down, what their role is isn't clear. Some look around, stressed. Others call out: Are there enough water bottles in the studio? Do all the chairs have cushions? Is anyone taking care of Mr. Rosada?

The longer Egbert looks around, the more he realises he doesn't belong here. It would have made more sense to meet Koen somewhere else. Together. Why do all these people have to be here too, why did he give in so easily? Now there's no turning back. The show has invested a lot in him, now he has to deliver.

The production assistant never leaves his side. She smiles when he looks at her, but Egbert sees only restlessness in her face. She's probably thinking about everything that still has to be done before the show begins. Or about what she hopes the guests will say, the outpourings, the slips-of-the-tongue, what do people want to see most on these shows?

She walks him to the television studio, a brightly-lit, windowless hall. It's smaller than he had expected. He had watched a few previous episodes on the internet — always two guest authors, usually one from the Netherlands and one from abroad. The conversations were too short to actually have any substance but long enough to appear profound. Occasionally a serious question, followed by a joke or an anecdote. Watching on his laptop Egbert thought the studio was quite large and pleasant. But now that he's here it seems to him more like a glorified waiting room.

To the side of the stage there's a gallery: twenty-five to thirty people, jammed together like a football crowd. The rest of the studio is taken up by a wooden table covered with newspapers. Egbert sees Koen sitting next to the host. They're having a lively conversation, the host laughs about something Koen says, Koen drums triumphantly on the table.

From a distance Egbert listens to what his son is saying: the well-intentioned commonplaces that roll from his lips, about an upcoming literary festival, about some trending 'poet in residence' who's always on TV. Then the production assistant abruptly pushes Egbert into his chair directly opposite Koen. 'You're the first item,' she says. 'When it's over, go sit in the first row with the audience.'

Egbert nods and looks across the table. 'Hello, bud. I made it.'

'Yo,' Koen says calmly.

The host sits down between them. He's wearing a grey suit and a red shirt and smells of expensive aftershave. With a firm handshake he introduces himself, but Egbert doesn't catch his name. 'I'm sure it's going to be a great show,' the host says. 'Let's not talk too much now, that'll only make it less spontaneous later. And, believe me, the viewers at home will notice.'

'On the air in six,' someone behind Egbert calls out.

The studio is filling up. The cameramen check their equipment, a technician fastens a microphone to Egbert's shirt, a director he can't see — or is it someone else? — shouts out the last instructions. Egbert wants to say something to Koen, even if it's only to say it's nice to see him again, just a small token of fatherly concern. But everyone in the studio is so silent and tense, Egbert doesn't dare to say all he wants, he can't come up with the right words anyway.

Four minutes till we're on. Three minutes, two minutes.

Everyone is ready. The host addresses the audience, he says he's so glad that they're all here, that he's really psyched up, that the Christmas special is one of the highlights of his year. He then purses his lips, looks at his reflection in the monitor in front of him and runs his hand through his hair. More lights are switched on, bright and close, what Egbert wants most is to shut his eyes and open them only when it's all over.

For a second no one says anything. Then, just before the cameras start to roll, the host suddenly puts his hand on Egbert's shoulder. 'Don't worry. As long as you smile convincingly everything will be all right. Ninety per cent of television is visual.' He utters these last words softly, as if it were just between the two of them, a shared secret.

The broadcast begins. Egbert has trouble following what's going on. First there's applause, surprisingly loud, then the host turns to the camera. He talks adeptly and quickly, the sentences follow each other in rapid succession without a pause for breath. 'Tonight, our guests: Koen Talan, the well-known family historian and author of the bestseller *Family, The Root of All...* — a, shall I say, very candid account, in fact, a settling of the score with his father. The twenty-fourth printing came out last week. High time to take a look at the background of this fantastic piece of work, and we do this with the two protagonists, together for the first time on television: the author and his father.'

'Settling the score' is not how Egbert would put it. 'Critical contemplation' is closer to the mark. The text is assertive, yes. The prologue, which was added at a later stage, is even downright harsh. But still, if memory doesn't deceive him, it mostly contains fairly matter-of-fact passages, views on modern society, researches into family affairs and present-day family life.

'I just want to say it's very courageous of you to join us,' the host says. He emphasises each word. 'You braved the journey from Brussels, you could just as easily have ignored the invitation. First question: What did you think?'

'About what?'

'The book. Your son's book.'

'A thorough piece of research,' Egbert says. But since that sounds a bit meagre, after a brief silence, he adds: 'Definitely very good for a thesis.'

'Yes, no doubt about that, but let's be honest, you can't judge it simply as any old thesis or book, of course. There are many passages in it about your behaviour and your role as a father. I can imagine you're not too pleased about that.'

A direct approach, Egbert saw it coming. This talk is less than twenty-five minutes, there isn't any time for elaborate introductions or cautious attempts at conciliation. At home, in the shower, he had thought about how he should react to direct questions like these. A few sentences about fondness and family ties, a few about the inescapable father-figure role. But now that he's sitting here, the words seem too predictable to him, too gutless. He tries to make eye contact with Koen, and when he doesn't succeed he turns to the host again. 'Of course, I would have preferred some things to have turned out differently. Who doesn't, at my age?' He stops talking. But no one interjects. 'No, I don't have any serious objections to it,' he says.

The host grimaces in surprise and turns his attention toward Koen. 'The book reveals that, to put it mildly, you didn't exactly experience your youth as pleasant. You recount, very poignantly by the way, that for years, to this very day in fact, you felt emotionally neglected after your father left home. It turns out to have been an unbearable deficiency, especially since your mother passed away, eight years ago. Is it difficult for you to face your father again?'

'To tell you the truth, yes,' Koen says, although he doesn't sound moved. With a flourish he reaches out and produces a book from under the pile of newspapers. It's thick, at least four hundred pages. *Family, The Root of All...* it says in shiny, gold capitals. 'This is the story of my youth, but at the same time, it's about every boy who was ever deserted by his father. That happens more and more often. My book is more than a personal story, it's a reflection on our times. Why so many relationships break up and so many parents fail to take care of their children.'

All of a sudden everyone looks at Egbert. Koen, the audience, the host, the cameramen, dozens of eyes focus on him. As if he'd been given the floor in court, a lawyer given the last chance to plead for his client's exoneration. But it's Egbert who's the accused. And how can he defend himself without knowing exactly against what?

He'd already explained it to Koen so many times. It was over. If he hadn't been the one to leave, then Marieke would have ended the relationship. They certainly didn't want a child. They weren't meant to have a child. But all of a sudden she was pregnant and now she didn't want an abortion, no matter how much Egbert insisted. She thought it was cruel. She didn't dare. She said he had no notion of how it feels, a living being in your belly.

'Of course I can't speak for other parents,' Egbert says. 'But I've never run away from anything. That's why I'm here.' There's absolute silence every time he speaks. No one says a word, no one reacts in any way. 'Believe me, if I really was as indifferent as the book suggests, I wouldn't be here.'

The title of one of the reviews was: 'Son strikes back mercilessly.' 'Strikes back — strikes back?' Egbert said to Alma, holding the paper. 'What do they mean strikes back — did I strike first? No.'

She shrugged, mumbled something about different perspectives, how everyone creates their own reality. Then she went out to eat with her girlfriends and didn't come back till the middle of the night.

For five long years they persevered, the two parents and their unwanted child. They lived under one roof and led a life similar to many other families around them. They picnicked in the park, played in the sandbox or drove to France in their Peugeot. But it was never more than pretence — half-hearted and unconvincing. Marieke thought he was detached. Inscrutable, she once said. Eventually he couldn't stand her any more. Her smell, her voice, her 'you knows' and her 'likes', everything got on his nerves from the moment she forced a kid on him. Their rows escalated, almost imperceptibly, until they were squalling at each other like second-rate soap opera actors. One evening, when he felt he'd completely lost his grip on the situation, when he'd had enough of the never-ending reproaches and when his son's baby talk wouldn't stop droning in his head, he made an accusation against Marieke that he had never expressed before, a remark that made all the other complaints seem insignificant: that she had used him to become a mother.

Marieke had turned around and walked out of the room in silence. Maybe she had hoped he'd come after her, apologise, change his mind, finally be one of the family. But he didn't.

From that evening on they hardly talked any more, only to Koen, the silent witness who was too young to understand exactly what was going on but old enough to realize that something was drastically amiss. A month and a half later Egbert decided to move. 'We can't go on like this,' he said. Marieke only said: 'You can't do this to Koen.' But he left anyway, to an apartment on the other side of the city. He wanted to come over on weekends to see Koen, but Marieke forbade it. 'You didn't want him,' she said. 'You're the one who walked out on us, you can't just come back whenever you feel like it.'

Should he have done things differently? Should he have threatened to sue, or demanded to be allowed to see his child once in a while?

He met his new girlfriend, Irene, a person with whom he felt immediately at ease. They lived together for years. They bought a house away from the city, in Voorschoten and even got married. It was fine like this, without the ballast of a child, without being saddled with responsibilities, just spending time every day with the woman you love. Until Irene was taken away from him. Just like that, in the middle of the night. A congenital heart defect she knew nothing about. In the evening she fell asleep next to Egbert, in the morning he awoke next to a lifeless body.

Marieke stayed in Amsterdam with Koen. He never heard from her after Irene's death. She didn't even send a card after the funeral, which unexpectedly caused Egbert much grief. As if ties with his first family, his progeny, were definitively severed, as if this was Marieke's way of letting him know that there was no connection any more between his current life and his former family. He let his contact with Koen, by now a reticent high schooler, slip away — they saw each other only on rare occasions, during awkward dinners, Koen only displaying anything resembling cheeriness once they went their separate ways.

Sometimes Egbert tried to imagine that it wasn't Marieke who had got pregnant but Irene. Would he have been more involved as a parent? Would a better marriage have made him a better father?

After Irene died Egbert travelled through Europe. This was unexpected, inasmuch as there were any expectations at all regarding his future. But to him it felt like an absolute necessity, he couldn't go on any more in Voorschoten, the whole country bore too much sorrow and too many silent longings. After months of roaming, during which he didn't speak with Koen, Egbert ended up in Brussels. He got a job there as a clerk and fell in love with his assistant, Alma. No wedding ring this time, no contract. He would call Koen only once in a while, out of a vague sense of duty, but the conversations kept getting shorter. It sometimes surprised him that he did so little to improve their contact. Sometimes he almost forgot he had a child. And as long as he didn't see his son he didn't feel like he was really missing anything. Of course it was too bad how things turned out between them, sad and disappointing. But Egbert was seldom gripped by feelings of guilt. It all felt too obscure for that, too unreal.

'Mr. Talan, did you hear what I said? If you keep this up, I don't think this talk will get us anywhere. You're sitting here next to your very own son, your clearly distraught son, you haven't seen each other for years and you seem, if I may say so, pretty... apathetic.'

The host looks hopefully at Egbert. Logical, the prelude has come to an end, Egbert has to show something. Pain. Sorrow. Resentment. Even out-and-out fury, as long as some kind of emotion is displayed.

But Egbert is not in the mood. He isn't here to do what the show wants him to, he feels no need to shed any light on his side of the story. No, the only reason he's here is because his only child had asked him to, had begged him to. Because 0.1%, no matter how many years he'd wait, no matter what he did, would never be the same as 0%.

'Why don't we take a look at this interview?' The host picks up a newspaper from the table, raises it so fast that Egbert doesn't get the chance to read the headline. 'A good, candid talk with your son, by one of our esteemed colleagues at *de Volkskrant*. It appeared last weekend, have you read it?'

'No. I was still in Brussels.'

'You can buy *de Volkskrant* in Brussels, too, you know. But anyway.'

Egbert senses that people in the audience are whispering. The host clears his throat and holds the newspaper closer to his face. 'I quote: "Even a father who makes mistakes and is never there can serve as an inspiring example. If I ever have children, I at least know what not to do. I know how important it is for a father not to be completely absent." I assume a quote like this doesn't leave you unaffected?'

'I could think of nicer things', Egbert says, his voice somewhat shaky. 'But a writer obviously has to have a convincing story. This isn't a complete representation of the facts, I talk to Koen on his birthdays, and we used to go to swimming lessons once a week, and quite often to football matches, and...'

'Wait a minute,' the host says and raises a peremptory arm, like a traffic officer stopping a car. 'Did I get that right? You dismiss your son's story as a sales pitch because you went with him to a couple of swimming lessons?'

It isn't a question, it's an opinion, on the provocative side but just short of being rude. Most guests would counter these kinds of accusations, wouldn't be able to stay calm and would lash back in full force. But Egbert doesn't want to get into a discussion with a host who's far more eloquent and who no doubt can argue more trenchantly, he mustn't let himself be needled.

Hesitantly, he looks at Koen. He searches for some kind of reconciliation, however slight, a trace of camaraderie. But the youthful, self-assured face across the table seems vague to him, distant too, as if Egbert were at home watching television.

'Let me put it differently.' It takes Egbert a few seconds to realise that the host is still talking to him. 'Did you ever consider the possibility that your son would come out with all of this? This story, I mean. After all, a large part of it is also your story, your life.'

Egbert shakes his head and the burning stomachache returns briefly.

'Really? You had no idea?'

Now Egbert is certain, there's talk in the gallery: soft, disapproving sounds coming from several ladies. 'I don't understand why you're making such a big deal about it. I mean, it's not so world-shattering, parents separate all the time.'

'That's why this book appeals to so many people. And there are all kinds of ways to abandon a child. You completely disappeared. Another thing: Do you think your son has the right to do what he did? You just said you don't have any "serious objections" to it, but do you think anyone should be allowed to write a book about their parents, just like that, without permission from the people in question, even though it's clear it all really happened?'

'Of course they should. People can write about whatever they want.'

Again the surprised grimace, you'd think the host wasn't capable of more than a couple of expressions. 'Does it bother you if I say I don't completely buy your comfortable attitude? For instance, Koen writes that you just up and left one day, without saying goodbye, and that you haven't made any serious attempts to stay in touch since then. Surely you're not unaffected by a passage like that?' And before Egbert can answer, the host says: 'No, I don't think so. And in another moving part it says that you weren't around when your son was suspended from school and, just after that, during his final exams, when he had to go to a child psychiatrist for months. Apparently, after you got married, you couldn't be reached at all.'

'Yeah, well, what can I...'

The host keeps talking without pausing for breath. 'How about if I go through the whole list? You've been living in Brussels for years and haven't invited your son down once. You have the tendency to not show up to the very few get-togethers you do have. You not only abandoned Koen's mother, your second marriage also hit the rocks, and the last time you spoke with your son was years ago. With all due respect, that doesn't exactly sound like the description of an involved father. Wouldn't you have preferred it if Koen hadn't disclosed all of this?'

Egbert swallows and, as another stab of pain shoots through his stomach, he sees Marieke's and Alma's faces before him. But he doesn't let it show. He's not going to be the kind of guy who suddenly goes all gooey hoping for sympathy, an emotional slimeball who uses his deceased wife as an excuse, inconvenient and hurtful as the host's choice of words may be. Egbert must stay strong, especially now, with all those eyes focused on him — Alma, Koen, hundreds of thousands of people are watching, this is his chance to show he can stand his ground.

'I don't really get what you're driving at or why you won't let my son speak for himself.' As he utters the last two words, Egbert taps the book in front of him. His fingers stain it with moisture. 'We were going to look at the book's background. Shouldn't Koen be part of the conversation? This has only been about me.'

Silence. The host turns over a sheet of paper on the table, and another one. Egbert doesn't let it get to him. It's rehearsed, this talk's buildup, the hospitality leading up to it, the bustle in the studio, the pauses, the amazement. Everything had been carefully orchestrated beforehand to elicit his reaction as effectively as possible, to cause a sensation, to boost ratings.

'If you don't mind, I'll stick to you for now. Because, what's it like for you to be here?' The host holds up his hand to stop Koen from talking. 'I mean: when you hear what he has to say, don't you feel sorry for him, or sympathy at least?'

'Of course, I knew there were problems,' Egbert says. 'Before and after I left Koen's mother.' Should he now say: I never wanted a child? Or: Maybe I would have been a better father, more involved, if I'd been with another woman, but Marieke didn't want me to see him any more. Could he say something like that about a dead person?

His fingers are now trembling, his hands, his arms. He feels the impulse to get up and run out of the studio. But he's held back by shame, a sense of duty, without exactly knowing what duty or to whom.

'Of course, growing up with only a mother is not an ideal situation,' he finally says. 'On the other hand: it happens to so many children. In fact, can you show me a family where everything's perfect?'

'Well, we're talking about *your* situation now. Excuse me for going on about it, but you seem to keep trivialising the past. What about the interview in the newspaper I just quoted: you have to admit this is a lot worse than "not ideal"? If my daughter said things like that about me in the paper I'd at least take a good hard look at myself. Do you understand why?'

What the hell does that mean: take a good hard look at yourself? What does the host know about how often and when Egbert did that? It's none of the audience's business. And why is Koen still looking so goddamn smug?

'I'm not proud of this book,' Egbert says. 'I am proud of my son's success, of course, but not about the content.' And then, after the umpteenth pause, he can't resist: 'If you ask me, it's also isn't a completely faithful representation of the facts, but that's beside the point.'

The host smiles, very casually, as if Egbert's remark was a joke, barely worth a laugh. 'Well,' he says, 'we could keep on talking but it's almost time for the next guest. Koen, what's your opinion? Your first encounter in years: is it liberating, is it nice seeing your father again? Or does it mostly feel like an unfulfilled promise?'

For a split second Egbert thinks the host is referring to him, that that's what Egbert is: the embodiment of an unfulfilled promise.

'I'm glad he came,' Koen says. 'Pretty courageous. Though one appearance on TV obviously doesn't compensate for twenty years of absence.'

'Hard words, but perhaps understandable. All I can say is: judge for yourself and read *Family, The Root of All...*, a wonderful book that will leave few unmoved. Gentlemen, I'd like to thank you both for this captivating and candid talk.' The host turns to the camera, switches to a slightly softer intonation and reads from the auto-cue. Egbert can see the text: 'And now, tonight's next guest. He's been tipped as a potential Nobel Prize contender and he's here in the Netherlands especially for our show tonight. His work is characterised by political reflections and modern...'

The production assistant motions to Koen and Egbert to leave the table without being seen by the cameras. They sit next to each other in the front row of the audience. Egbert wants to say something but obviously can't while the host is speaking. There is applause, the Argentinian author appears, a small man with grey hair and a tight-fitting custom-made suit, Egbert realises he just saw the man backstage.

The Argentinian takes Koen's seat. A conversation in English begins, Egbert has trouble following it. He has the feeling that the rest of the audience is watching him. He peeks at his son out of the corner of his eye, he tries to read his face, no idea what he's looking for.

While Mr. Rosada speaks — in fluent, seemingly endless sentences, he says something critical about the current Argentinian drugs policy — one of the cameras turns toward Egbert. He has no idea whether he's in view and tries his best to watch the conversation as attentively as possible. The pain in his stomach flares up, one sandwich is really not enough for a whole evening. He rubs his stomach unobtrusively. He massages his muscles to calm himself, and just as he's about to finally concentrate on the interview he hears music coming on. A soft saxophone melody, delicate piano notes. The host thanks his guest and looks at the camera again. Talking quickly, he declares that the show is over. He announces who the guests will be on a different show next week, a show he apparently also has a role in. Egbert doesn't know who they are.

And then it's over, although it seems to Egbert that the actual confrontation is still to come. Up to now if felt like a preparation, his own talk as well as the Argentinian's. He'd exchanged three sentences at the most with his son, not more than in their emails, tentative and without touching on anything meaningful.

Almost everyone stands up at once. The host slaps the Argentinian writer's shoulder and mumbles something cheerful about the show, worn-out words that you can tell he's often used before, that have more to do with the program than with the actual guests. Then he gives Egbert and Koen the thumbs-up. 'We did it,' he says. The audience walk to the exit, the soundmen fiddle with their equipment. Sweaty hands are shaken, you can hear people saying things like 'interesting show' or 'spectacular shots'.

Egbert stays in his seat and wonders which of the conversations are about him. 'Do you think it went well?' he quickly asks before his son gets up and disappears into the crowd.

'I think it was good TV, yes. The second guest was interesting too.'

'Good TV,' Egbert repeats tonelessly. 'OK, yeah, that's also important.' He looks aside at his own blood, the stranger who will live on in his name. 'Are you well, too, by the way?'

'What?'

'How are you? Doing OK? Are you happy with your success? Are things going the way you hoped?'

'Sure. Yeah, doing good. Thanks.'

As Koen gets up, Egbert hesitates over whether he should say more. Is this the right moment for intimacy, for apologies, for everything that was left unsaid during the broadcast? Egbert wants to say something about the past, a meaningful detail, a crucial insight. But he can't think of anything. Looking back on the past twenty-five years, on his time with Marieke and his years without Koen, he can't put his finger on any big mistakes or key moments that he would have handled differently today. All he sees is a string of occurrences that couldn't have gone any other way, simply because that's the way they went.

The audience leaves the studio. The newspapers are taken off the table, the cameras are rolled away, in the foyer drinks coupons are handed out. People are drinking beer, wine, tea and coffee. Egbert joins the crowd. His job is done. He has become part of the promotion campaign. The face behind a faulty upbringing. And due to that face, thousands of copies will probably be sold in the coming weeks.

Did you watch the show? he texts Alma. *What did you think? I didn't make an ass of myself, did I?*

Egbert stands at the bar for a while. He tries ordering food but it's impossible, they only serve drinks. A woman of about sixty accosts him to say she thought it was a captivating interview. 'Very intriguing. In every aspect, in fact.'

Egbert ignores her. He looks at Koen, who's caught in a conversation on the other side of the room; two middle-aged men are listening attentively to what he's saying. The host comes back, no longer in his suit but in jeans and a shiny brown jacket. He shakes hands with almost everyone, says how much he enjoyed it, to Koen, to several members of the team, and then to Egbert too. 'It was great having you here. I hope to meet you again.' The host then walks off without any elaborate farewell, he just shouts *'ciao'*, goes out and disappears.

After that the foyer quickly starts to empty out. As though no one knows what to do when the host isn't there. Egbert walks over to Koen, a soundman goes to them and asks whether father and son want to have a beer with the producers. 'I can't,' Koen says. You can hear complacence in his voice, it aggravates Egbert's nausea. 'I have to give a reading tonight. In Abcoude.'

Egbert declines too. Why would he go, except out of politeness?

The people exit, one by one. At the door the production assistant hands Egbert a bottle. The wrapping paper is bright red with drawings of Christmas trees. He unpacks the bottle right there. To his surprise, it isn't wine but olive oil. There's a card attached to the bottle: *Thank you for being with us.* Signed by the same network CEO as the chocolates.

Some of the team walk into a side street, apparently that's where the show's local haunt is. Egbert and Koen stay put.

'Are you sure you don't want to have a drink somewhere else?' Egbert asks.

'No, I really have to go.'

They take a few tentative steps. There is no car waiting for Egbert in the parking lot. Not that he was expecting it, there's no more need for him to be put at ease, the show is over.

'What are we supposed to do with this olive oil?' he asks after a brief silence.

'Dunno. You want my bottle?'

'No, thanks.'

Koen holds out his hand. 'Well, thanks for coming. I have to go now, I'm already running late. We'll email, OK?'

Egbert watches in silence as his son goes. When he's a couple of yards away Egbert takes out his cell phone. Still no messages. He calls Alma. She doesn't pick up. Maybe she's already asleep, she often goes to bed early these days. He doesn't leave a message, puts the phone away and raises his arm to wave to Koen, the self-confident, youthful figure that keeps getting smaller.

In the meantime he tries to figure out how to get to Leidseplein. Through the parking lot, following his son or maybe the other way? What difference does it make? Amsterdam isn't *that* big, at a certain point he'll get to Leidseplein anyway. He'll get a hamburger or something and chew on it while walking, as his body slowly calms down and his hunger finally subsides. At the hotel they'll be waiting for him, friendly, albeit less friendly than a few hours ago. Maybe there will be someone else behind the counter, a new receptionist, a night porter. Hopefully they won't know who he is and will let Egbert walk past quietly. In the worst case they'll say something unctuous about the broadcast: not bad, stood your ground well. Whatever they say he'll smile politely. In his room he'll try to relax by watching the sports news or a movie, but he'll make sure to turn the TV off before the book show comes on again. And very early tomorrow morning, when almost everyone is still sleeping, he'll walk back to the station. Through the city centre, across the canals, the sun only just peeking over the rooftops. Egbert's feet will leave a shallow, quickly-fading trail in the slush. He'll take the train to Brussels, still practically empty at that hour. He'll eat a pre-packed sandwich again, watch the Dutch landscape go by, stop at identical stations. A couple of hours later, when the day has just begun and the first people are on their way to the office, he'll arrive in Brussels and walk home. With every step the interview will seem more alien to him. At home he'll go to the bedroom, unpack his suitcase, put away all his clothes, lie down quietly beside Alma and caress her hair. She'll mumble something. Back already? Was it fun? But she won't wake up or ask any more questions. He'll gaze at her for a long time, she's prettiest when asleep. And when he's certain she can't hear him, he'll ask: 'Are you happy I'm back home?'

From afar Egbert watches his son step into a shiny, dark-grey car. He keeps waving even though he can't tell whether Koen can still see him. His right arm moves back and forth mechanically. As if he were being controlled by someone else, as if this is the last thing he still has to offer his son. After all those years, it all culminates in an outstretched arm in an old factory.

He waves to Koen as his son fastens his seatbelt. Less than 0.1%. He waves as the car's engine starts, he waves to the shut windows, the windshield wipers that push away the snow, he waves to the taillights, keeps waving till there are only two red dots in the distance.

nieuw new
dutch **nederlands**
stemmen voices

VERZET is a series of chapbooks showcasing the work of some of the most exciting writers working in Dutch today, published by Strangers Press, part of the UEA Publishing Project.

Each story is beautifully translated and presented as an individual chapbook, with a design inspired by the text in collaboration with The Dutch Foundation for Literature and National Centre for Writing.

1 **RECONSTRUCTION**
   by Karin Amatmoekrim trans. by Sarah Timmer Harvey

2 **THANK YOU FOR BEING WITH US**
   by Thomas Heerma van Voss, trans. by Moshe Gilula

3 **BERGJE**
   by Bregje Hofstede trans. by Alice Tetley-Paul

4 **THE TOURIST BUTCHER**
   by Jamal Ouariachi trans. by Scott Emblen-Jarrett

5 **RESIST! IN DEFENCE OF COMMUNISM**
   by Gustaaf Peek trans. by Brendan Monaghan

6 **THE DANDY**
   by Nina Polak trans. by Emma Rault

7 **SHELTER**
   by Sanneke van Hassel trans. by Danny Guinan

8 **SOMETHING HAS TO HAPPEN**
   by Maartje Wortle trans. by Jozef van der Voort

Supported by
N National Centre for Writing
N ederlands letterenfonds dutch foundation for literature

This series was made possible by generous funding from The Dutch Foundation for Literature